The Primates of Woodpeck Ridge
and
Other Ramblings

Elmer McCoy
and
J. Carol McCoy Phelps

PublishAmerica
Baltimore

© 2008 by Elmer McCoy and J. Carol McCoy Phelps.
All rights reserved. No part of this book may be reproduced, stored in a retrieval system or transmitted in any form or by any means without the prior written permission of the publishers, except by a reviewer who may quote brief passages in a review to be printed in a newspaper, magazine or journal.

First printing

With the exception of "Little Friend" and "The Obituary," all characters in this book are fictitious, and any resemblance to real persons, living or dead, is coincidental.

PublishAmerica has allowed this work to remain exactly as the author intended, verbatim, without editorial input.

ISBN: 1-60610-462-4
PUBLISHED BY PUBLISHAMERICA, LLLP
www.publishamerica.com
Baltimore

Printed in the United States of America

Dedication

To Phyllis, Gene, Kyle, Kimberly, Karen, Keith, Jim, Gina, Mary Ruth, Susan, Bob, all their significant others, and to all their children. We love you more!

Acknowledgments

We gratefully acknowledge the contributions of and say thanks to the following: Phyllis, for typing the early stories on a manual typewriter and for sheer endurance; Gene, for moral support and the patience of a saint; our kids and grandkids for their encouragement; Myra, for letting us use Smiley as our cover girl; the beings and places that inspired our characters; Blue Sky Photography (www.bskyphoto.com) for our photograph; and most of all, we acknowledge and thank our gracious Lord and Savior, Jesus Christ.

Table of Contents

The Primates of Woodpeck Ridge, by Elmer McCoy
* 9 *

Home in Time, by J. Carol McCoy Phelps
* 21 *

God of the Chosen One, by J. Carol McCoy Phelps
* 37 *

Little Friend, by J. Carol McCoy Phelps
* 41 *

The Obituary, by Elmer McCoy and J. Carol McCoy Phelps
* 49 *

The Primates of Woodpeck Ridge

The sun turned its face away as it sank past the craggy prominence of Woodpeck Ridge. A typically dreary evening, it was as though after eons of desolation, light would have to be reflected in from a more joyous place. Decades of coal mining stripped the ridge of any natural beauty it may have once possessed, blanketing everything in sooty tones of gray. Even the sun loathed looking upon this barren land.

The old man existed from day to day. If he was hungry, he trapped food. If he wasn't, he didn't. He would sometimes fish in Little Pine River, which also served as a septic service to several small towns northward. He drew his water from the river, whose twisted path and stench commiserated with the gloomy landscape.

He had arrived there a vagabond, on the run from a trail of broken hearts and countless outdated support payments in the arrears. Having grown accustomed to his personal misery, he probably couldn't have lived without it. The place mirrored his own depression, so naturally he loved it in a morbid sort of way.

Upon his arrival some 15 years earlier, he erected a crude dwelling. A builder he had never been, but he went about his work, and an occasional satisfied sigh would hiss between his gapped teeth. Rough hewn timbers, notched and stacked at odd angles, provided a certain comical pitch to the structure. One room, one door dragged in from an old refrigerator by the side of the road, one window covered with a canvas tarp and one dirt floor defined the questionable boundary between indoors and outdoors. Some minimal protection from the elements was the only luxury the shack provided, but it sure beat jail…and marriage.

His wardrobe consisted precisely of two red plaid shirts, two denim overalls, a red union suit, and a coat. He didn't like having to spend time deciding what to wear. If he was cold, he wore the union suit under his clothes and his coat over them. If he was hot, he didn't.

Sometime in the old man's tenth year of residency, a mongrel reddish brown dog happened onto the stark home site. Neither he nor the old man wanted him there, but the dog was hopelessly lost, and the old man was too afraid of him to try to shoo him away. Some ancestor in his mixed heritage contributed an under bite that made Dog look meaner than he actually was. The old man and the cur wearily settled into a mutual friction that erupted into occasional fang baring and swearing. Both too old and tired to fight to the death, they ate, slept, bickered and survived in the utter absence of anything resembling a partnership. Undercurrents of animosity as ugly as the cabin itself marked each waking moment of the ill-matched pair. Their association suited their environment.

The old man had been suffering increasingly distressing stomach attacks when he noticed Dog eating some leaves. Dog was cunning and clever, and not to be trusted at all, so this could be a ploy. After days of carefully calculated reasoning, he decided the animal was also suffering and wasn't just trying to trick him into eating something poison.

So, he gathered some of the same type of leaves and ate them. A bitter but minty flavor nipped at his tongue, but he'd eaten worse. Daily. Although his pain didn't completely leave, it eased to a more bearable degree.

As time passed he experimented more and more with leaves, grasses and roots. He kept faithful records of the ingredients and stored his potions in the glass jars he found drifting randomly downstream. He rigged a vine across the stream just above water level at an angle so that the debris would wash ashore. He collected what he wanted, then knocked the rest under the vine with a stick and squatted down to wash his cache. The water being a foul purée, washing anything was basically a remnant from his mother's teachings and some small gesture of good intentions on his part.

Once, while boiling some sweet-smelling brew, he noticed changes in the insects that flew over the blackened pot simmering on the wood stove. A mere moth would suddenly attack a bumble bee, and win! "They may be deadly poisonous," he thought. "What if I breathed them vapors?" His paranoia took charge and fear gripped his scrawny throat with great, deadly talons. Holding his breath and summoning all his courage, he carried the container to the corner to cool.

The next morning when he awoke, a creature about the size of a rat lay beside the pot. It had more scales than hair. Its head bore strong, muscular jaws and long sharp teeth.

"Don't believe I ever seen anythang quite like that before," the old man mused, glad that his potion had killed this hideous monster before it could get to him. Somewhere in the back of his mind, the thought nagged that Dog was a completely useless biscuit snatcher. The lousy mutt didn't even as much as whimper during the night when that thing was skulking around in there. He had neither the courage nor the vigor to kick the sorry beast.

Truly glad he'd discovered a new secret weapon, he busied himself bottling his "demon killer" and putting drops on the scattered chips from the firewood he dragged in from the forest. That, he reasoned, would keep anything from coming down the chunky stone chimney to get him. One day while he sat resting, a small mouse nosed one of the wood chips, licking away the sweetness. The mouse dropped as if dead. A change began immediately and wasn't even complete before it was a dead ringer for the beast he had found beside the pot. When the old man poked the creature with his walking stick, it attacked the end violently. "Vicious little knocker," the old man chortled, beating it senseless with the stick. "The first one musta got a tad too much," he noted.

The appearance of the animal brought to mind the drawings he had seen in books of the evolution process. "Have I really learnt how to put things back like they usta be," he queried aloud. Dog ruffed a vexed and most contemptuous contradiction to such an absurd theory. Ignoring the dull-witted critic, he continued making the "demon killer" while generating and then exterminating an array of odd-looking creatures.

Solitude cultivated a deeper paranoia. He was convinced that any human who ventured near had come for the sole purpose of capturing him. He dreaded being dragged back into society to face the women and children who each wanted a scrap of his contemptible hide. They would lock him away, or worse. Although he couldn't imagine what would be worse. Before discovering his "demon killer" he would run and hide when he suspected company, although no one ever came all that close to the shack. But now he defiantly plotted and planned while cooking the brew. "If I can just fool 'em a leedle bit. Jes' get 'em to take one leedle sip. They'll never bother me again."

One day he peered out into the stillness to an unfamiliar noise. A hunter blundered onto the homestead. Other than being tired and thirsty, he had no interest in the place or its occupants.

"Would you care for a leedle swaller of my demon killer," he politely offered, extending a jar.

"What? Don't mind if I do," the hunter laughed. "I'm lost anyway." The reddish ruff around his mouth lifted upward at the possibility of sampling some bona fide hillbilly brew.

The old man passed a jar across the threshold of the open door.

His lips curved slightly into barely a ghost of a smile just before he snapped the door closed.

"Well, how do you like it," was the muffled query from inside the cabin.

"Not bad. Little on the sweet side," the hunter answered from the yard where he assumed the coal miner squat beside Dog. Beefy fingers with raw, ragged cuticles scratched droopy flea-bitten ears. Dog's lone response was a resigned, "huff." He remotely recalled the hunter smell, and in some odd way it almost comforted the old creature. He closed his eyes and drifted into a long-forgotten dream of flushing out rabbits in a sweet, distant field in a sweeter, more distant past. Presently one back paw twitched and Dog's sides heaved in tempo with canine-dream whimpers.

A bushy eyebrow twitched close to a crack in the wall near the door. He could faintly make out that the hunter was still vaguely recognizable, but rapidly changing into an ape-like creature of sizable proportion with silvery fur and deep-set, dramatic red eyes. He slumped in a sleep-like state with his shotgun still across his thighs.

The old man was sure the thing would soon be after him. He wanted to run out and shoot it with the shotgun. "But, what if it wakes up before I can snatch the gun?" his frantic mind warned. "Oooh, gaaaa," he whined, wringing his frail, bony hands. In his panic, he remembered the hole he had dug out back for privy privileges. "It will never look for me down here," he promised himself, sliding the stump he used to cover the hole back into place over his head. His long-standing acquaintance with Little Pine River rendered him immune to the stench in the honey hole.

A blood-curdling scream out front triggered Dog's frenzied, staccato yips that faded in the distance as it topped Woodpeck ridge for the very last time. Tedious silence engulfed the old man as the ape bounded up the hill. Still, he waited until after dark before sneaking down to the river to wash off—yet another exercise in futility that he insisted upon repeating.

In following months, sightings of the odd-looking, red-eyed apes spread about the county, as did the missing persons reports. Rather than keeping people away, the old man's plan had backfired and he was overrun with unwelcome visitors. Other hunters, hikers and clandestine lovers—curiosity seekers all—succumbed to the invitation of the "demon killer." Nervous gossip and the most sincere journalistic efforts of weekly newspaper reporters theorized that the apes were eating folks at an alarming rate.

Hysteria swept the nearby towns as local police forces combined to dispatch a task force to exterminate the flesh-eating apes. They met at the mouth of Take-In Hollow to plan their strategy before starting the trek up to the foot of Woodpeck Ridge. A young deputy spat out a jagged shard of fingernail as he related a rumor that an old hermit had built a cabin up there, as well as a small bridge across the river. The bullet-proof vested chieftains decided the posse would cross there and spread out to initiate their offensive.

Bullet proof vests? Had there been a rumor that the apes had guns as well as an appetite for human flesh? Oh no. They knew their cohorts all too well. When bullets start flying in those hills, the likelihood that any shooter is taking careful aim decreases in proportion to the number of guns and the number of bullets being fired. At least, that's true in deer season.

Rumbling footfalls and shrill banter belied the fear gnawing deep within jittery stomachs as the posse neared Woodpeck Ridge. The footbridge swayed and crackled under their thunderous crossing. The sight of a gnarled old man with what they thought were several jars of hillbilly brew at the other side of the bridge took them by surprise. Shaggy beard and thin, greasy, stringy hair that hadn't seen the benefit of a blade in many years shocked the modesty of the more well-groomed members of the posse. Yet, they found him amiable, even jovial, as he offered them "a leedle drap o' courage before the battle." Soon, the jars lay empty and the lawmen awoke to discover first-hand that gorillas are vegetarians. The colony gained a dozen new members that day, all of whom were shortly relieved of their tendencies to be alpha males.

The townspeople waited uneasily for word to come of the demise of every last ape. Days passed, and eventually there settled a dark cloud of acceptance that the combined forces had lost the battle, and the lawmen would not return. No one braved to explore the woods for quite some time thereafter.

As the ape reports spread, a state university anthropologist commenced preparations to go in to study the creatures. Since their reputation was that of highly intelligent flesh-eaters, and tales of narrow escapes abounded, she decided to go alone and not risk any other lives. She had to see for herself natural apes in America, apes that had to have been there for who knows how long, carnivorous apes at that, and discover how such a large colony had gone completely undetected until recently. University officials were not at all in favor of her trip and refused authorization; but, the lure of a newly discovered species was too strong to abandon.

With a borrowed four-wheel-drive, field glasses, khaki walking shorts and her favorite mauve lipstick, she drove purposefully to the area. Parking the vehicle at the mouth of Take-in Hollow, she scanned the brushy slope and chose what appeared to be the most promising path. She checked her knapsack for essentials including insect repellent, snake-bite kit, camera, notepad, nail file, and comb and picked her way through the forest. Within the hour, she found her way to the bridge.

The old man standing at the other side of the old bridge startled her. She was prepared for an ape, a monster, or even a hangnail, but not a human! A forbidding cold chill zipped down her spine her as she scanned her surroundings.

"Whew! What is that smell?" she asked, setting her supplies down on the bridge and making a mental note to bring some "Pure Allure" eau de cologne on her next excursion.

"The river," he answered, sauntering into her personal space of less than arms-length. Lewdly eyeing her lithe 35-year-old frame resurrected a fleeting memory of feminine secrets but, alas, after but a brief moment, it scurried to the back of his thick old skull where it hunkered down meekly. Glazed eyes returned to clarity as his focus shifted back to his task.

"Care for a leedle 'freshment?" he asked holding out a jar of liquid.

"What is it?" she asked cautiously.

"Call it m'demon killer," he returned with a hint of pride in his voice.

"I don't drink," she retorted, a properly upturned nose glistening for lack of powder.

"Not al-kee-hol," he explained.

"What's in it?" she asked, loosening a bit.

"Jus' herbs," he offered, "s'been a long, hot walk, what with totin' all that stuff."

"Yes, it has and if it is herbal tea, I'd love some. Say, do you ever see any of the apes from the ridge?"

"Matter of fact I do, time to time. 'Spect I'll be seeing one real soon too." A shadow of a sneer punctuated the sentence.

She ignored it. The place would definitely take some getting used to, she thought as she took her first sip. "Ummm, sweet too." Then her second. "Tastes exotic." Then her third. "What's that odd flavor?" she asked, enthralled.

"Could be the water," he laughed.

"Where do you get your water," she demanded, paling at the anticipated reply.

"The river," he laughed, pointing to the murky ecological defilement.

Now, good breeding and years of proper manners commanded one never to spit in public, but she spat. Several times. She wanted to gag and puke, but this her refinement would not permit.

As she felt her consciousness fading, dancing eyes tried to converge on the leering vermin before her. Lacking full cooperation from her tongue, she demanded thickly, "What have you…dunth thew me, you ole cooth?" She melted into a delectable little khaki and blonde tidbit on the wide-spaced bridge slats.

The old man retreated to what he deemed a relatively safe distance at the other end of the bridge to watch the transformation, having lost most of his fear of the primates. They had long since proved to a man, or ape, to be wholly disinterested in him.

Heavy eyelids lifted slowly, unveiling scarlet eyes where once gleamed the wit and intelligence of an educator; where once shone the will to force any issue she deemed worthy to any extent she thought necessary. Now, a mere distant cousin to her former self, those eyes were home to blandness and animal urges for colony life.

The wrenching scream that arose from the massive head sent the old man tumbling off the bridge into the river in a revival of sensible caution. Several primal bellows answered from the ridge, and she scampered off up the mountain. Somewhere in a neat and distant condo, sixteen pairs of assorted leather pumps with matching handbags, countless mix and match outfits in austere earth tones, and an arsenal of beauty products awaited distribution to a local charity thrift store. Somewhere a former male suitor mourned the loss of his four-wheel drive vehicle.

In the wee hours, the old man sat in his self-imposed exile listening to the moonlight shrieks and screams of hopeful males vying for the attention of the newly arrived female. Jagged yellow fingernails probed a couple of itchy places on his back as he prepared for bed. Habit dictated that he missed Dog, but not that much and he knew he'd get over it. Miscellaneous transient thoughts skittered around in his brain long into the night.

"Bet if I was up there, I could teach 'em a thang or two…" With this, true inspiration elbowed its way to the forefront of his consciousness. "The law would never expect a go-riller to pay child support," he crowed, grasping a dingy jar of his potion.

With one large gulp of the "demon killer", the old man eyed Woodpeck Ridge, awaiting the inevitable with a full blown smile on his lean, sallow face.

Home in Time

Jack's nostrils flared slightly as he sampled smog-free air. The corners of his mouth leapt upward, pointing merrily at his dancing brown eyes. The town was alive, with people coming and going in all directions. A buckboard clapped happily past in perfect tempo with this un-orchestrated symphony of the song of life.

Across the street, low and sprawling, Morgan's Mercantile and Ma's Boarding House modestly awaited their patrons. Toward the east end of town, a glistening white steeple pointed souls to God. The majestic spire rose slightly higher than the belfry of the plain clapboard schoolhouse just beyond. From the west, the dry wind carried faint echoes of the blacksmith's rhythmic ching-chinga-ching, upstaged only momentarily by the soprano aria of a steam locomotive's whistle. "Perfect," Jack breathed the word. Everything was exactly the way he had hoped, no, prayed, it would be. If this were a dream, he wouldn't pinch himself. Still, it was very real, of that he was certain.

Dr. Jack Parker, relieved and enthusiastic, drank in the

atmosphere, his eyes devouring the sights around him. Dr. Whyte had been precisely right: this, 1884, was the time for Jack. It looked right and it felt right. He'd made it! He was in Dodge City. He had at last found his home in time, the one he had yearned for all his life.

Just to be sure, Jack had to ask a lady who was exiting the mercantile, "Pardon me, ma'am, what is today's date?"

The round face flushed softly beneath a calico bonnet as a melodious voice answered, "It's Tuesday, June 10." Then she swished away, skirts rustling at her ankles, twine-bound packages crinkling in her arms.

Still, he needed more information. What was the year? Jack felt a lump rising in his throat, and then he caught sight of a newsboy. Edging closer, he read the date on the Ford County Globe: Tuesday, June 10, 1884. A chuckle exploded past the lump in his throat, erupting into gales of laughter. People were beginning to turn and stare, but Jack didn't care at all. He had beaten time! He had traveled 124 years into the past. A hundred years' weight lifted from his shoulders in that instant.

Hurrying to an appointment, Reverend McCoy hesitated long enough to stuff a dollar into the pocket of a vagabond's tattered shirt. "Have a nice day, doc," he said softly. Then he hurried on, hailing a taxi as he stepped off the curb. No one knew who the old man was, or had been, but he was always jolly, and altogether harmless. In this part of town, a few people gave him food or pocket change almost daily. The old man babbled endlessly to imaginary acquaintances about their ailments. The regulars along the busy street would nod or smile in return as they went their busy ways.

There were many like him. It seemed they were on every street corner, and growing in numbers. He was one of the many homeless people, the have-nots, touching a few hearts, hoping for no more than a day's meager subsistence from some, and expecting no less than the indifference and neglect doled out so generously by the rest. This was 2008, the time Jack Parker had chosen to abandon because he preferred to take his skills as a physician to the Old West.

To him, the city was like a gargantuan garbage truck, noisily scattering its overfill as it rattled and banged through the streets. The homeless were bits of refuse, tossed by the wind, kicked aside by the throngs that had things to do, places to go, people to see.

"They come and they go without mercy, with no one to mourn their passing," he had told Dr. Whyte.

Dr. Sherrill Whyte glanced at his Rolex, stirred his coffee and sipped. His small stature and tufts of silver playing at his temples cut no imposing figure. He could have been anyone's father, having lunch before returning to the soft fluorescent lighting of an office that more often than not shielded his pale countenance from the sun. The sidewalk café, though, was his favorite meeting place in fair weather; and today, June 10, 2008 was beautifully clear and warm. He reveled in the melodies of the city, smiling inwardly that he was about to make another dream come true. Dr. Whyte loved 2008 and would not even entertain thoughts of living in a different time, but, there were others.

At 12:04 a yellow taxi eased toward the curb to discharge a dignified gentleman in a gray three-piece suit. He emerged, squinting, one hand shielding his searching eyes. Scanning the army of faces, he swept the cupped hand into a transitory salute of acknowledgment, and strolled to Dr. Whyte's table.

Dr. Whyte rose slightly, offered his extended hand, and the two men exchanged polite greetings. A silken breeze tickled the silver fringes of the umbrella, dipped down to tease Dr. Whyte's napkin, then danced casually to the next table.

"What a glorious day for a trip," Dr. Whyte mused, as if speaking only to himself.

"Doctor," the gray-suited man began, "you are certain that it…that this, um, trip, is safe?"

"Mr. Thornburg, we've covered that. However, if you are still in doubt, perhaps you shouldn't go. I told you that I shall place only those who are physically and psychologically fit," Dr. Whyte spoke flatly, rising in preparation for departure.

"No, wait! I am ready, unquestionably. It's just a case of last-minute jitters, I assure you," Robert Thornburg pleaded in desperation.

Dr. Whyte lowered himself back into his chair, confident he had won another one for all time. "Do you have the portfolio?" he asked, lowering his voice.

Robert pushed the portfolio across the table, "Everything is in order. The house keys, my personal credentials, and the cash. I don't understand how you will transfer…"

Dr. Whyte raised a hand to silence him. "We shall not discuss this again. I have certain contacts and have made the arrangements. You need know nothing more," Dr. Whyte replied tersely. A meticulous man, Dr. Whyte perused the contents of the portfolio to his satisfaction before making the offer to proceed to his office for the final stage of the transaction.

"Hold my calls," the doctor instructed Miss Morgan as he and Robert strode past her desk and beyond the open, ornately-carved oaken door into his posh office.

"Now, Mr. Thornburg," Dr. Whyte spoke firmly, "you are certain that you have told no one of our arrangement?"

"Positive. My secretary and business associates think that I am going away for a month to take a much-needed vacation."

"You have left behind no clues that would lead back to me when you fail to return? You are aware of my personal risk in this matter, and you have protected me from suspicion once the authorities declare you a missing person?"

"Absolutely. Your identity will not be compromised. Your name is nowhere to be found in any connection with me. Besides, I can assure you that I kept my therapy strictly to myself."

Robert Thornburg left Dr. Whyte's office exactly 15 minutes later, proceeded to Dulles Airport, and boarded a jet for New York City. From La Guardia, a taxi took him to Fifth Avenue where he stepped out of 2008 into 1900.

In 2008, Robert Thornburg's secretary took messages that would not be retrieved and scheduled appointments that would not be kept. The senior partner, Brad Myers, posted a memo in the lounge instructing staff to direct to his office all correspondence or inquiries related to Thornburg's pending cases.

Robert Thornburg's disappearance was of consequence only to those who worked in the small law firm, and that only for a short while. He left behind no family and no close friends. Amid a few, "Tsk, tsks," and little flourish, Robert was unceremoniously replaced and his personal belongings put into the hands of the Commonwealth of Virginia. Indeed, he was only one of multitudes who vanish, and was thus hardly a ripple in life's torrid stream.

Robert dashed into the alley where he expected to find the valise. He needed the clothing and money of the period to start his new life in 1900. Unlike Jack Parker, Robert focused his interest first in getting settled. He'd have the rest of his life to savor the changes he could see and the adventures he was sure to encounter.

Robert saw the corner of the valise where it lay, hidden beneath some discarded wooden crates. "How did he do this?" Robert mused as he delighted himself in the contents of the valise. He found a tailored brown suit, complete down to the smallest accessory, even wire-rimmed spectacles and a silver-fitted monocle on a sterling link-and-leather fob. His credentials appeared to be in order, and there was every cent of his seventy five thousand dollars in the proper currency.

After a quick change, Robert burned his 21st century clothing, his final tie to 2008, and strutted out of the alley to see if he could find the address on a small card in the valise—his new home. Robert walked with a proud and dignified gait, lightly doffing his dark fedora to the ladies. He barely refrained from humming, "East Side, West Side, all around the town," as he took in the sights and sounds of this great city in its youth. Yes, he would fit in here, and he would make a name for himself. It would, however, be a bit of a different name, as he had acquiesced to change Thornburg to Harris, at Dr. Whyte's insistence.

Watching the numbers closely, he finally confidently tapped the brass door knocker on the stately brownstone. When the butler appeared at the door, he received the card, "Robert J. Harris, Esquire, Attorney at Law."

"Do come in sir, we've been expecting you," the butler intoned, bowing deeply as he spoke. Robert deposited the monocle in his inner vest pocket, grandly swept his hat toward the waiting hand, and crossed the threshold of promise.

Amelia lay rigidly against the cool Italian leather of the psychiatrist's couch. Night terrors, haunting half-memories of some unspeakable childhood horror had broken her. Driven to contemplating suicide, she at last fled to the sanctuary of Dr. Whyte's cool, dimly-lit office.

"His hands," she whimpered, "I can see his hands. They're cruel and always so cold. I can't cry. He forbids it. He's, oh, no! Daddy, please," her whimper strengthening to a wail, "oh, please!"

"One, two, three," Dr. Whyte whispered. "How do you feel, Amelia?"

Brushing back a wisp of mousy brown hair, she sat up. Her

fingertips traced the wetness of her cheek, prompting the question, "I've been crying, haven't I?"

Dr. Whyte nodded in assent.

"I…feel…relieved, I guess. Did I…did I tell you who?" she asked haltingly, soberly, eyes downcast.

"Yes, you revealed your abuser. But, I don't feel you're ready, Amelia," Dr. Whyte continued, "Perhaps next week."

"No! Tell me! You tell me now! I dream, I see hands, but not a face, never the face! Am I crazy? Am I just imagining it all? Are you just playing me along to keep me coming here?" Her delicate fists pummeled the edge of the couch.

"Amelia, you are not crazy. You have suffered a delayed discovery of childhood abuse. This is not at all uncommon. You…" Dr. Whyte was speaking as Amelia interrupted.

"I understand about repression," she hissed. "Just tell me who. I want to know who the monster was!"

"My dear, you must trust me," Dr. Whyte cooed, clasping her flailing hands.

"Stop patronizing me! If this hypnosis therapy revealed something about my past, I have the right to know," she began furiously, but crumbled in racking sobs.

Amelia buried her face on Dr. Whyte's shoulder and sobbed several decades' worth of pent-up tears. Silently, he held her until the storm subsided.

Accepting the tissue he offered, Amelia apologized, "I'm sorry. I usually control myself. This isn't like me at all." She sniffled, her face red as much from embarrassment as from her outburst, and continued, "Of course I trust you. If you think it best, I'll wait. Still…" her voice trailed off, following her gaze out the window and beyond the confines of glass, concrete and steel. What could she hope to see out there? Just the empty, lonely nothingness that stalked her, its icy fingers clutching at the dark side of her soul, threatening to consume her from within.

"Next week we'll see how you're doing. Just trust me," Dr. Whyte smiled disarmingly. Had Amelia been less focused on herself, she would have noted an alarming lack of warmth in that smile. It was as artificial as the light of the fluorescent tubes gleaming coolly within the recesses of the sunless ceiling above.

"I will, I mean, I do," Amelia answered weakly, contorting her features into an attempted smile as she gathered her things to leave.

Watching Amelia exit past the oaken door, Dr. Whyte's smile faded to a somber, more natural expression. "Yes," he made a mental note, "Amelia would like to escape this life and go to a different and better time." Still, there was no hurry. He had mastered time.

Two months later, Amelia languished in the discovery that it was her father who had brutalized her as a child. He had died years before, so she couldn't even confront him to release her rage. It made her hate him all the more. Therapy appeared to be helping very little, and Amelia found it even more difficult to function day by day. Dr. Whyte worked her carefully, and methodically, aware that the moment to introduce her to time travel had come at last.

He offered Amelia a chance to start over. She could travel to the past or to the future. Live anywhere, any time. She embraced the concept eagerly. She had only a few thousand dollars left to her by her grandmother, but reasoned that she could be quite wealthy if she went back to the 18th century.

"Yes," Dr. Whyte explained, "if you will bring the money to me, I can arrange for the transfer to currency of the time and place you select."

Although too excited to care about minute details, Amelia had to ask, "How?"

"It's better that you do not know too much," his voice took on a darker tone, "for your safety. Just the slightest slip and you could be executed for witchcraft."

Trusting Dr. Whyte with all her heart, Amelia followed his instructions to the letter. After withdrawing all her money from her bank accounts, she carefully checked her apartment. She thoroughly searched and destroyed all bills, receipts, appointment cards and such that linked her to Dr. Whyte.

On the appointed day, Amelia dressed simply in a tee shirt, a long loose gauze skirt and sandals, and abandoned all clues to her identity. She left Cassie, her pound cat, with the neighbor across the hall, saying that she was going to visit relatives in North Carolina for a few days. Mrs. Humble had kept Cassie before, and agreed it a good idea for Amelia to get away for a few days. The twinkle in Amelia's eyes and the spring in her step gave Mrs. Humble a warm glow as she closed the door.

Cassie liked Mrs. Humble as much as a cat can like any human. With all due cat pomp and circumstance, she circled regally and then curled up on the old fashioned blue and pink floral sofa to purr herself to sleep. Mrs. Humble gathered her knitting back onto her lap and resumed the important business of counting stitches. Neither Cassie nor Mrs. Humble realized that they would grow old together waiting for Amelia, who would never return.

Amelia's smile curled downward as she stepped onto the train for the short ride from Vienna to D. C. Her mood blackened as she passed all the people who didn't know her and didn't want to. "You wouldn't care if I were starving in the streets," she thought bitterly. "But, it doesn't matter now. Soon, very soon, I shall be a rich and powerful lady. You won't know it, but I will." From the train, she took the escalator to the 15th Street NW exit and walked up to L.

Amelia's expression softened the moment she rounded the corner to see Dr. Whyte sitting at the sidewalk café. Had anyone cared to notice the abrupt change in her countenance, they would have smiled spontaneously at her glowing joy.

"It's twenty two thousand," Amelia whispered as she slipped the stone-washed denim knapsack to the ground at Dr. Whyte's feet.

There was no need to interrogate Amelia as he had Robert. He knew she was ready. Following a light lunch of shrimp salad and tropical fruit for dessert, they proceeded to Dr. Whyte's office. Holding his young patient to his stately pace, he felt no need to hurry despite Amelia's obvious zeal.

Entering Dr. Whyte's suite, Amelia was startled to see everything draped, with cartons strewn about in various stages of packing. "What in the world…" Amelia gasped.

Miss Morgan was rushing about, screeching instructions to the movers. She glanced at Dr. Whyte and Amelia only briefly before returning her attention to the care of the rubber tree plant one of the men was struggling to move, hindered more by her interference than anything else. All the activity reminded Amelia of an ant farm—so much hustle and bustle within uncompromising impediments to progress—and she couldn't help saying so, with a giggle she hadn't used in years.

Dr. Whyte shushed Amelia's comments until the oaken door heaved a sigh, snicking closed behind them. "I'm moving to a larger suite across town," he answered in anticipation of the question that marked itself on Amelia's brown.

"Lie down, Amelia," he instructed. "I must put you under one last time to ensure that your subconscious has retained the information necessary for your transition."

Amelia, as serious as she had ever been in her life, wordlessly settled back for this final preparation. She closed her eyes and let the luxurious sofa cradle the beginning of her dream come true. No shred of human decency remained in Dr. Whyte, or he would have felt at least some compassion for this tiny figure with the long, silken brown hair.

Once deep in the hypnotic trance, Amelia became Dr. Whyte's one-hundred-fourth victim in and about the D. C. area. Since the early 1990's he had plied his trade, dispersing his victims across several major cities, so there were hundreds of them altogether. Instead of final instructions on language and customs relative to her time placement, Amelia was prepared for displacement in her own time.

"You will recall nothing about me or about your present identity. You will call yourself Lady Elaine. You will see and hear London, England, 1702. When cars pass, you will see and hear horse-drawn carriages. You will block out sounds foreign to 1702. You will eat scraps you find and believe them to be prepared and served by your own peerless chef. Alleys and abandoned buildings will be your grand palace," Dr. White droned.

Growing richer all the while, he prided himself in secretly upstaging the infamous suicide doctor. His patients would die also, eventually, but they would die happy, living out their wildest fantasies to the last breath. Truly, he had a warped view of himself as their savior. They were dead already, and he gave to them the lives they desired. In return, they collectively gave him untold wealth, which he spent lavishly. He could go on for years without getting caught. After all, who could accuse him?

Even Miss Morgan was under his spell, subconsciously suppressing all memory of clients who were purged from the records at Dr. Whyte's command. He could steal and leave no witnesses, no complaints—the perfect crime. There were some clients who escaped, having lost nothing more than a few bad habits and minor emotional distress. He needed these people as a shield. They thought he was a miracle worker. Oh well, he needn't be greedy, right?

He finished Amelia's sentence to her mental prison with, "You will know where you are until you pass through the entrance at the airport. At that moment, you will leave the airport, and take a taxi to the bus station. There you will purchase a ticket to Chicago. Once you exit the bus, you will believe you have arrived in London of 1702 to begin your life as Lady Elaine. You will go through the motions of seeking and finding a valise in which you expect to find period clothing and money. You will happily live and converse with persons you shall imagine to be your family, friends, and servants."

"When I count to three and snap my fingers, you will awaken, but you will not recall anything I have just said to you," Dr. Whyte spoke slowly, and deliberately, "One, two, three."

Amelia opened her eyes and smiled at Dr. Whyte. "I feel so refreshed, like my whole life is about to begin anew. Thank you Dr. Whyte, I'll never forget you," she promised. Turning to exit, she beamed a cheerful, "Good day," to the movers and their ever-present queen, Miss Morgan.

Dr. Whyte didn't like her making such a spectacle of herself in the presence of so many potential witnesses, so he grasped her by the elbow and steered her into the hallway, keeping his body between her and the men who were too busy with Miss Morgan to notice anyway. "Don't expose your thoughts to another living soul until you arrive in 1702," he seethed once they were out of earshot.

"Oh, I'm so sorry! I just feel so good. Oh, Dr. Whyte, I promise, I won't call any further attention to myself. You'll see. I'll just disappear quietly," Amelia pronounced her destiny with a truth she couldn't begin to fathom.

The new sign reflected the glow of the southern sunshine as Miami gained another citizen, Dr. Sherrill Whyte, Hypnotherapist. The population of the city ever increasing, he would scarcely be noticed. Before long, a few compassionate souls would shake their heads and occasionally remark, "There are so many more homeless people these days. Someone should do something, but they come and they go in such rapid succession that it's impossible to even find out who they are." Dr. Whyte's homeless, indeed, were at the mercy of the elements and other people because of their inability to communicate outside their time-prisons.

In a Chicago park, some children laughed merrily and played one of their favorite games of chase. They paused momentarily, tossing popcorn at a ragged young woman who curtsied before strolling away arm-in-arm with an invisible companion, engaged in lively conversation. "How you do go on," Lady Elaine coyly replied to her suitor's compliment on her newest gown.

Meanwhile in Memphis, a gaunt, shabby man was about to undergo hypnosis in the care of a psychiatrist. The doctor recognized the poor creature as the Baltimore lawyer who had handled his divorce a few years ago. Although he insisted his name was Robert Harris, the doctor was certain he was talking to Robert Thornburg. This good doctor would attempt to reverse whatever process had plunged this gentleman to such a piteous existence. If he failed, he would see to it that Mr. Thornburg was institutionalized as a matter of mercy. If his attempts were successful, he hoped for nothing more than to restore the man to his place in society.

At this moment, neither of them could imagine the horror they were about to explore, nor could Dr. Whyte.

God of the Chosen One

Today marks the beginning of my many years of training to become a High Priest. My parents are proud. Father does not speak as he walks ahead, leading the family to the place of my confirmation. He does not look at neighbors who stop what they are doing to watch us pass. This is a solemn occasion and he looks only at the path before us. Although he does not speak it, I know his heart is bursting with pride, for I am a Chosen One.

In all the times past there were no other Chosen Ones in my bloodline. We Chosen Ones are not like the others. Our skin is different and our hair is different. I am like my mother, but females cannot become High Priests.

My childhood has been one of privilege but also one of remarkable responsibility. Father trained me in the ways of manhood and I am strong and agile. Now that I am in my 16th year, the High Priests will take over my training. I will live with them in the temple, never to cross my parents' threshold again.

We make the journey to see the god today. I have not seen the god before but Father says he once did as a child. It is forbidden for any but the High Priests to look directly upon the god except at the time of a confirmation. It was such a time when Father hid in the bushes and gained a privileged glimpse of the holy one. His chin quivered and his eyes grew misty whenever he spoke in hushed and reverent tones of that great event. Today he shall look upon the god again. This is something few men do even once, much less twice, in a lifetime. Father is envied by all in the village. His son is a Chosen One, and he shall see the god for a second time. He will be treated with the greatest respect after today.

There, in the distance, rise the gray walls of the temple. It is an ancient structure that dates beyond our recorded history. Ruins of other temples, of brown and gray, are evident here and there. This was a mighty, holy city at one time. I feel a lump in my throat as we grow nearer the awesome site.

In the heat of the day we stand before the great door. Father announces our arrival and is answered from within the great walls. A rumbling like distant thunder sends prickles of fear scurrying down the back of my neck as the great door begins to rise and magically disappears into the top of the wall.

I have never seen a High Priest before. As the first one emerges, we dutifully bow down before him. After the blessing we are allowed to stand and face the High Priests. Father taught me these rituals. I know exactly what to do.

The High Priests are not dressed as we are in the spare clothes of the common people. The High Priests are in the ancient garments reserved for those who attend the god. Those ancient garments are delicate and are now worn only for ceremonial purposes. One day I too shall wear the High Priest's garment.

Father speaks the words of submission and the Priests accept the gift of the Chosen One. As my family turns to leave, I do not look back. My father taught me well. I know exactly what to do. I wait for the Priests to welcome me further into the temple where my training begins today.

All of my years of preparation make me confident that I know how to behave and what to do. Yet, fear and excitement make it difficult for me to retain my composure. Suddenly I feel like an ordinary child, not like a Chosen One at all. The great door reappears and rumbles down.

I stand before the god. His glistening skin is the color of fire. It is the color of my hair. Now I understand why I am a Chosen One. My hair is the color of the god.

As instructed, I touch the cool, hard skin of the god. I am surprised. I thought it would burn like fire but it does not. It is cold. It feels lifeless, but I dare not utter my thoughts. A High Priest hands me a ceremonial cloth and shows me what to do now. This is the secret ceremony that none but the priests know.

One priest applies a soothing balm to the skin of the god. The rest of us move with great dignity but great vigor as we use our ceremonial cloths to wipe the balm away, leaving the god's skin glistening.

I remember the stories of my childhood that one day the god

would come to the village and carry us all to paradise. No one knows just when that will happen, but we know it is true. We know this because our fathers and our fathers' fathers have passed on the legacy of the Great Redemption.

My long day is nearing an end and the priests lead me to my pallet near the god where I join the circle of vigilance. We sleep with the god and we care for the god. This is to be my life until the Redemption, or my life's end.

The balm is near me. I am curious because of my youth and now I pick up the container. An older priest sees me do this and just smiles, so I know that it is all right for me to look. I do not understand the symbols on the container. It is said that no one does. While I cannot tell you what these symbols mean, I can make them for you. The symbols are "Armor All."

Little Friend

Several times, I looked under the loveseat, and even turned it over to see if there were a rat or something inside! It all started when we purchased a love-seat from an antique furniture dealer; thereafter, things were never again the same. Shortly after moving the loveseat into our home, I occasionally felt something moving under the loveseat, pushing up on the end where I sat. Sometimes, it would shake the whole loveseat. Other times, it was so light that I could hardly feel it. I accused Pete of teasing me until it happened one day when he wasn't even home! It wasn't Pete's toy poodle, Killer, because he was usually on my lap or lying right beside me. This was the beginning of an odd, but loving experience with a mysterious entity we eventually dubbed "our little friend."

The next manifestation was my favorite. While I was hospitalized for chest pains in late December, my daughter, Susan, bought me two large Mylar balloons: one was heart-shaped and bore the message, "I love you," and the other was round with a "Get

Well Soon," message. For several days after I returned home, the balloons remained attached by thin pink and white ribbons to a small flower vase sitting on the kitchen table. As they aged, the balloons began to sink under the small weight of the ribbons, so I cut them free.

For about a week, the balloons hovered against the ceiling above the table. Then, one day, I asked Pete, "Where is the heart-shaped balloon?"

"I don't know!" he said, shaking his head.

We looked around the kitchen and in the living room, which was separated from the kitchen only by a short, low counter projecting from one wall. There was no sign of the balloon.

"How could something that big and colorful just disappear?" I asked.

"I have no idea," Pete replied.

"Did you hide it just to tease me?"

"No, I haven't touched it."

A couple of days later, upon rising from bed, I heard something brush the wall or ceiling in the corner above a built-in chest of drawers where Pete kept his clothes. It was the missing balloon! There were no open windows, there was no discernible air current as even the furnace was not on, but the balloon was bobbing, as if dancing, in the corner.

With a smile, I left the room to join Pete for morning coffee in the living room, intending to tell him I had found the wandering balloon. When I entered the kitchen, though, Pete looked at me, actually past me, with a wide-eyed, open-mouthed expression that made me stop in my tracks. "What is it?" I asked.

"You've got somebody following you," he replied in a hushed tone.

Turning around, I laughed out loud. That balloon had followed me out of the bedroom, down the hall, and into the kitchen, staying back about three or four feet from me and right about eye-level, instead of up at the ceiling where it had been in the bedroom. My balloon followed me into the living room. Its antics amused us all day. At times it would bob and dip down in front of me as I sat on the couch. At other times it would go back down the hall and into the bedroom or bathroom. In short, it was all over the house. It would "hide" behind the counter and playfully pop up at me as I passed by, as if playing peek-a-boo. The odd thing is that the round balloon remained in position over the kitchen table all this time. Another odd thing is that the traveler did not play with Pete. However, he enjoyed it whole-heartedly.

For several days, we continued to be amazed as the balloon moved about the house. Then, one morning as I entered the kitchen, Pete said with a grin, "He's gone again. I've looked all over and can't find him."

I went back to the bedroom, but the balloon wasn't there. Just as I re-entered the kitchen, it popped out from under the table, right up in my face, then it sallied around the room and joined the round balloon near the ceiling over the table. Such frolic went on well into the spring.

Around Father's Day, Pete had gone to visit his sister and I was cleaning the living room. The weather was fair and clear, so I opened the door for some fresh air. Killer immediately bolted into the yard for a good romp. I looked at the little heart-shaped balloon, resting above the kitchen table, and said, "Why don't you go out and play with the other kids for a while in this pretty weather?"

No sooner were the words out of my mouth when the balloon zipped across the ceiling, bobbed down, turned its "I love you" side toward me for just a fraction of an instant, and swished out the door. I felt a twinge of sadness, watching it rise and float gracefully out of sight. I thought it might return, but we never saw it again. The round balloon remained where it had been all along, but the helium had weakened a lot, so it was resting on the table rather than floating around. I had left it there all those months as a point of reference, somehow proving that the heart-shaped balloon was not just floating around on air currents.

However, other mischief began to take place. One night, Pete and I were watching television. He was sitting on the end of the couch near the dividing counter. Against the other side of the counter was the kitchen range. For a brief moment, I caught a glimpse of something out of the corner of my eye. It looked like a great puff of smoke or steam had risen from the range and dissipated quickly. Although I did not want to say I'd seen something, I peered in that direction, trying to determine what it had been. Pete asked, "What did you see?"

To be sure I wasn't going nuts, I asked him, "What did YOU see?"

"You'll think I'm crazy unless you saw it too. But, I saw a puff of smoke over the stove," he replied hesitantly. We both went to the stove. It was cold. We laughed about this, because fear was never a factor when our little friend asserted itself.

Through the spring, then the summer, and even into winter and the following spring, it became quite usual for one or both of us to catch a glimpse of movement in the kitchen only to find nothing there. Several times, the dials on the washing machine turned as if someone were setting a cycle. Once, the dryer started on its own.

Killer was really nervous at first and would whimper or growl during a manifestation, beginning with the inner thumping of the loveseat. For a time he refused to stay in any room alone. But he eventually grew accustomed to our visitor and paid it no mind.

Susan and her husband, Greg brought Sparky, their large dog, over for a visit just after Thanksgiving in 1996. He romped in the living room with Killer for a while. Then, I threw a sock ball into the kitchen. Killer chased it all the way. Sparky ran too, but he stopped abruptly at the divider counter. He crouched low, staring intently into the kitchen. The hair stood up on the back of his neck, and he maintained that crouching position, growling at first, then barking viciously. This gentle giant of a dog was clearly alarmed. Pete and I explained to Susan and Greg that Sparky sensed our little friend. They laughed nervously but said they did not believe us. However, even after calming Sparky, they could not coax him, couldn't even drag him, into the kitchen.

During these months, our little friend began getting into bed with us. It happened to Pete first, then to me, then to us together. Even in broad daylight, if either of us lay down on the bed, it would be only moments before the bed would quiver slightly with the distinct sensation that someone or something small were climbing up over the foot of the bed. Sometimes it would settle down, other times, it would wiggle around and nudge my feet until I scolded it and told it to go to sleep. It always, always, minded me when I told it to behave. It wasn't Killer, because he invariably jumped up on the bed before we could get to it, then he would lie down near the pillows.

Once, I hung a plastic grocery bag by the handles over the back of a kitchen chair, planning to use it later for something or other. We were sitting in the living room, so I saw quite clearly what happened. The bag was snatched off the chair and thrown to the floor with considerable force, audibly crinkling the plastic. This was not a gust of wind or anything like that. All we could do was shrug and laugh. After all, that was a childish prank to get attention, was it not?

Whoever or whatever it was definitely had a sense of humor, and it gave us both much joy. It's difficult to tell people about this experience because so few believe. However, there were just too many things going on for it to have been our (and the dogs') imaginations. Anyway, Pete, in advanced stages of emphysema and constantly on oxygen, didn't feel quite so alone when I was at work. When I arrived home each evening, he delighted in telling me what all he, Killer, and our little friend had done all day. For Pete, there was a sense of peace and indescribable comfort attached to this presence.

Our little friend was a daily caller until Pete went into the hospital in June of 1997, where he died just a few days later. It left when Pete did, and I have had no visitations since. Rational judgment defies an explanation, but, I wonder whether this could have been Pete's angel, comforting and befriending him in his last days. I further believe it teased me so much because, first of all, Pete did too. Secondly, I think it teased me so that both of us would believe its presence and so Pete would not be afraid. I count myself blessed to have been permitted to share that sweet, funny, sometimes silly, but always gentle presence, Our Little Friend.

The Obituary

3 January 1992: "It is with fervent hope for whatever years remain before judgment that I am compiling this chronicle. If there are to be descendants in my blood line, I want them to know from whence they shall have come. In 100 years, I hope to be more than a dimly-recalled name."

Jcarmc sat before her monitor, oblivious to the signal being sent to Medfour. The journal she had recently acquired from a lunar library completely consumed her thoughts. The writings of this ancient ancestor of two thousand years ago aroused in her a passion that tore at the very fabric of the pain free society that she knew.

The words leapt off the screen, or so it seemed to jcarmc. In these few ancient pages, penned more than two thousand years ago, survived the spirit of a distant ancestor. The words were alive. Jcarmc marveled that the blood of those ancients coursed through her own veins. Discovery of this obscure legacy slammed into her soul with the force of a hurricane, awakening primal forces beyond her scope of comprehension.

She read the genealogy easily enough. The writer, Carol, was youngest of nine offspring. She cataloged the names and birthdays of her siblings, parents, grandparents and great-grandparents. As such, this part of the journal was similar to other historical documents kept in the archives.

The passages that riveted jcarmc to her seat, however, examined relationships, love, hate, mistakes, sorrows and joys. For jcarmc and her contemporaries, the course of 2,000 years of re-civilization had systematically eliminated the causes, and effects, of emotionalism. Long forfeited, such abstractions are no longer referenced. Now, trembling hands turned the pages of a past powerful enough to reach 2,000 years into the future and clutch her heart with strong, supple fingers of…emotion.

> "The children of the future should know I play piano and guitar and write songs. They should know that I like chocolate and looking at the stars."

"Yes, Grandma Carol, I want to know you, to remember you," jcarmc whispered softly. She turned a few pages and read on about a cabin in the woods where her ancestors vacationed.

> "If I close my eyes, I can hear the echoes of the tree-barking, the gunshots, the men whistling for their dogs, and the silence that enfolded us as the oil lamp burned low and the fire in the wood stove crackled into embers. Even that generation of dogs has passed on. So, too, will these memories when the last of us has gone. Deep snows, crystal frosts, pixie rains clicking their heels on

the tin roof, and the lofty sighs of tall timbers slapping back at the mischievous winds still woo the cabin. The forest hasn't noticed our gradual disappearance. Neither has the moon that always sends slivers of gold through the back window. Spider webs and bird nests are the decorative effects that a master designer has quietly slipped in, reclaiming the site as the forest's possession. Where once trod booted feet and fuzzy paws, now is seldom heard a human voice. The ritual of the winter hunting season, for Camp McCoy, expired with the founders."

Without comprehending how or why, jcarmc understood the beauty described, although even the natural elements were now in complete control of the society. Terra-forming covered the natural earth. Far below, bio-bots maintained the delicate balance of water and the inner shell ecosystem. While jcarmc's society would never see the actual face of the planet, lush foliage was carefully cultivated not only for aesthetic appeal but also to produce oxygen.

Terra-form was more efficient than the uneven terrain of the planet. Its level surface posed no problems for builders. Roads being unnecessary, and all bodies of water covered, there was plenty of room for structures to house the population as well as the plethora of equipment needed to sustain the environment.

Foreign droplets of moisture squeezed past her eyelashes and trailed down her cheeks. Jcarmc was not sure, but from things she had read, she thought she was crying. She knew, too, that it was only a matter of seconds until Medfour would transport her for treatment in the Asian facility.

Life and health now perfected, and with advances coming daily, the human tenacity for living conquered sickness, aging, and even death itself. Implanted on the inside of the pelvic bone, a place of virtual anonymity, a micro-chip transmits signals to Medfour of biological, physical, or emotional changes. By relaying computer-generated code to any given citizen's chip, necessary biological changes create healing before sickness has a chance to originate.

Abruptly, with her trademark "oh puh-leese" expression, jcarmc began to roll her eyes as she felt her molecules begin to disperse. Instantaneously the process transpired, and the eye roll was completed within the Medfour Asian facility. Problems are usually corrected without the need for on-site visitation. However, this was the hardest of cases, partly because of the lack of experienced caregivers in emotional issues.

"Jcarmc," the familiar voice reached her ears before they completely materialized.

"Yes, genphel, how are you today?" she responded. "Why are you speaking instead of projecting?"

"It is because of the new directives based upon research findings. While telepathy is the normal and most efficient method of communication, Medfour prefers to speak orally to the people they transport. Studies show that conversation eases apprehension," he replied.

*THE PRIMATES OF WOODPECK RIDGE
AND OTHER RAMBLINGS*

"Are you OK? This is the third time this month. What is wrong?" he searched.

"To be honest, a little over a month ago I was with some friends. We were playing a trivia game and began to discuss our curiosity about our progenitors. Wondering about my ancestry, I decided I would try to do a background search. Consequently, I discovered that my lineage was a very real family. There was a mother and a father...and children, all living in the same house. Sometimes they laughed, sometimes they cried, and sometimes they fought.

They, too, were interested in their origins. Researching the archives in the Lunar Library, I was even able to access a journal that was kept by one of my ancient grandmothers, whose time was at the dawn of the technology age.

In her culture she was expected to make the decisions about her future, and her daily life. Often they were wrong, but that strengthened her and she learned more by bad choices than the good ones it seemed." Jcarmc wept again softly as she continued. "The words she wrote—well, they make me cry. They are sad but, well, beautiful. Nothing ever has been so touching. I actually feel her despair as well as her capacity to...love. It puzzles me, love, that is. She wrote as though it was desirable, yet it seemed to have caused more sadness than joy."

She wiped away the tears, dabbed at her nose, then leaned toward the caregiver, and said almost as if in secret, "In another time that could have been me. I'm just so glad I'm of this society. Life back then was harsh!"

"You should read no more," genphel stated firmly.

"I know but…I can't…stop," she replied choking back more tears.

"Now, now," he said as he moved to her side and placed a comforting hand on her shoulder. "It's not as though you've squandered the world budget on the Jupiter moons…again." She looked at him quizzically as he turned and walked to the keyboard. Eyeing the big monitor she watched curiously as he keyed in some gibberish.

"There! I've changed your DNA. You're not related to this person anymore."

Her laughter reverberated in the stark cubicle, "Are you that dumb, or do you think I am?"

Genphel, to hide a smile, quickly pivoted, pushed a button, then glanced back to see her disperse, preferring that they could have continued the conversation. He busied himself at his work station, pushing thoughts of jcarmc aside. He would not be summoned before the elders on this issue again. He had learned to pace himself after her visits, to control the irregular rhythm of his heart. Both genphel and jcarmc were frightened of the strange attraction they shared, although neither ever mentioned it to the other.

Among the advances of the society, there were some sacrifices as well. Intimate relationships between the sexes were long ago abolished because of the complex issues involved. Citizens had become more productive in their work since the wildly swinging pendulum of emotion was stilled. The urge to mate was previously dictated by the species' survival instinct. For centuries, all births have been carefully controlled in laboratories, producing only a few births every few decades. Therefore, the species survival is not an issue. The seven elders, deemed the most intelligent of the human race, are the donors. Eggs are harvested from the top-ranking females, such as phigacon. The combinations are quite limitless, given the limited number of children produced.

The few unfortunate individuals who are incapable, or unwilling, to conform to the society's rules are promptly listed in the obituaries.

Back at her work station, jcarmc was unable to regenerate her passion for finding another galaxy into which the earth could be propelled. At this particular moment, smashing into the sun might not be such a bad thing. She mumbled, "I've got to get away from this."

As instantly as the mind wished it is how quickly she sat in her dinette pushing the button to make her selection. Within seconds she was eating a delicious, healthy, no-cal, no-fat dinner. She didn't particularly enjoy it this time, though. Her mind was a mess, and her emotions were working overtime.

Upon summoning the domestibot to clear the table, she arose and mentally connected to the person with whom she usually shared feelings. As she readied for her bath, she projected, "phigacon? Are you busy?"

"Yes but that has never prevented either of us from contacting," phigacon thought secretly. Then she projected to jcarmc, "What are you doing j?"

Phigacon prided herself in her self-proclaimed ability to keep her secret thoughts from those with whom she communicated, and was not always kind with these "secret" thought waves she unwittingly sent out. The people with whom she often communicated found this trait amusing and never let her know that she had a very open mind.

"Oh I was transported to Medfour again."

"What for this time?"

"The same old thing."

"Careful girl. Don't end up in the obits," phigacon warned.

The obituaries are the only form of death left to mankind. Upon the defeat of natural death, a council of elders was formed, one from each continent. If the council determines that a person is a threat to the pain-free society, his/her name is published in the obit section of the news com, with seven days to report to the closest council for dispatch.

"Surely that would be way extreme," jcarmc quickly answered.

"I don't know, remember vorbclee. And what about Lisa? Poor dear, with a name like that...no wonder." Phigacon countered.

"Yes, but they were intrusive communicators, always bothering people, and they were into doing weird stuff with the computers. Those bizarre chain letters they were sending around wasted too much time and were counterproductive."

I would have helped the council with those two." They both smiled in agreement. "Well I've got to get back to my spreadsheets and your water is getting cold."

*THE PRIMATES OF WOODPECK RIDGE
AND OTHER RAMBLINGS*

The very idea of bath water getting cold, where did phi get these thoughts? Jcarmc knew it was phigacon's way of breaking off contact to get back to her number crunching. But, cold bath water? How impossible!

The bath could wait just a little while longer. "I've got to stay away from Grandmother Carol," jcarmc promised herself as she pulled up the family tree. Reading about the people in her bloodline, she came across more of Carol's words, "When my oldest daughter came home and announced that she had joined the Army, I was too stunned to discuss it at the time, so, that night, I wrote this song."

Jcarmc saw there were words and music. "Play," she commanded the computer. A hologram of a balladeer with an acoustic guitar appeared and the ancient song1.mid file filled her room.

> The evening sun leaves mellow rays
> Playing in the shadows of the trees.
> The air is crisp and cool,
> Tempered by the early morning breeze.
> It's been a day like other days:
> Some things were right and some were wrong.
> But the news that came this morning
> Has made this day seem a life time long.
>
> My little girl is going away.
> She's chosen to join the ranks
> Of the free and the brave.
> Her heart is on fire for the USA.

Now she's going to leave me,
God, protect her, I pray.

My mind is filled with memories
Of Brownie troops and traveling with the band.
Bikes and dogs and first prom dress
Fade as I reach to hold her hand.
The little girl forever gone,
A woman now stands in her place.
With love for her country
Shining like a beacon from her face.

I guess that I should be proud
That Mary Ruth has grown to be so strong.
I taught her to respect the flag
And carry high the torch of freedom's song.
But I still see a little girl
Bringing me daisies in the spring.
On silver wings she's leaving me behind
With my memories of these things.

Jcarmc was at first mesmerized by what she heard in the haunting, simple melody. It conveyed sadness and apprehension, but also it revealed deep, deep love and devotion. Then she almost panicked, "Why is this music not allowed?" She queried, "What harm could it do? Who could this hurt? Why have they stopped us from listening to it?"

"Hold on girl," she told herself, "do some research." For the next several hours she worked diligently, scrutinizing all information available at her clearance level. She found no trace of any clue that society had been purposely manipulated in any way regarding the evolution of music. Still, she was wary, and wondered if she were missing something. She did not trust the elders on this issue. The question keeping her perplexed was, "Why would anyone listen to soft computer-generated instrumentals or the alternative, animalistic screeching of the contemporary genre when there was music that touched the soul so deeply?"

Suddenly phigacon interrupted, "jcarmc, have you finished your bath yet, dear?"

"No, didn't start yet, but I welcome a break. How are your computations," jcarmc prodded.

"Accurate. Listen, I've been thinking, why don't you come to work with me? This is a good job and it would take you away from all that scientific mumbo-jumbo involved in transporting the earth out of the sun's gravity. That's too much responsibility for you," phigacon offered.

With a broad grin on her face and in her sweetest and most patient projection, jcarmc declined such a worthwhile offer and laughed softly. Realizing the late hour, she left her desk and bathed quickly. She then plopped into her "Orion's Belt" floating bed. "If I had a mom, I would want her to be phigacon," she told herself, and yielded softly to slumber.

"Ooooooh, woooooo, ooooooh," echmol's high soprano wafted from the music room. Jcarmc pulled a pillow over her head to drown out her companion's pre-dawn aria.

"Echmol!" she called out, "put on the mute mask!" The song faded into silence as jcarmc flounced around, unable to go back to sleep.

As jcarmc stared into her second cup of coffee, echmol padded into the kitchen and stopped at the dispenser for a long, refreshing drink of cool water. He peered up at jcarmc and yipped excitedly, "I finally finished that composition. As soon as I score the accompaniment, I'm sending it to my agent. I smell another hit!"

With her trademark eye roll, jcarmc burst into laughter.

"What," echmol demanded. His large brown eyes bulged in perplexity.

"My dear, dear little friend! How did I ever get a singing toy poodle?" she gasped through waves of giggles. "My ancestor's dog howled some, but no one considered it music."

Offended, echmol tossed his long, silky ears and sniffed, "And your ancestor would not consider that caterwauling you do in the shower as music either. Who has the recording contract, sweetheart?" Daintily coifed tail in air, he pranced off toward his studio, perfectly manicured toenails clicking sulkily on the tiled floor.

"Come see me," she coaxed several times. Only because he still possessed—much to his chagrin—his species' attribute of loyalty did the tiny dog oblige. She leaned over, scratched the little black head and cooed playfully, "Oh, don't get your kibbles in a twist. I've been reading my family history. Two thousand years ago, your species was not evolved beyond howling at the moon and playing fetch."

"Fetch, indeed!" echmol growled. He recoiled and scampered back into the studio to finish his composing. Jcarmc stifled another giggle as he muttered, "Well, your species still scratches le derriere just like mine does…so, who has shown the more marked improvement here?"

Moments later the tiff was forgotten as echmol placed skillful paws on his electronic keyboard to record the melody tracks of his newest composition, "Tiny Puddles." To jcarmc, it sounded like all the other contemporary music—one piece almost identical to the next. What made echmol so popular was that he was one of the few musically inclined canine's who could both sing and play. Additionally, his vocabulary was far superior to any other dog yet discovered on the planet. This, no doubt, was because his human engaged him in scintillating conversations on a regular basis. Whereas most humans remained indifferent, jcarmc was fascinated by canine intelligence. Echmol had an engaging personality as well, which contributed to jcarmc's desire to see how far he could be developed.

His eclectic artistic style was beginning to cross over into the human genre, and was gaining popularity in the feline market as well. In one interview, echmol conceded that it was a strategic move to include "My Back Fence Baby" on his latest release, which was the song that garnered the attention of the truly hep cats.

Breakfast and the ritual morning row with echmol behind her, jcarmc transported to the office and again returned to her work.

"How do I break free of the sun's gravitational pull?" she pondered. There was no doubt that the earth was being slowly maneuvered closer to the sun. While there was no imminent danger, the prognosis was grim. It would take perhaps another thousand years for the earth to be destroyed, but it might also take that long to discover a viable solution.

"While it is theoretically possible to transport the earth out of the solar system, the propulsion of such a large mass scares me." She stared blankly at the monitor for a moment. "I wonder" she mused, "Would it be possible to create an energy shield…to negate the force of gravity within its periphery? Hologram," she commanded in a short, confident tone, never doubting the immediate appearance of a visible solar system bound only by the confines of the lab.

She walked over to the holographic earth and followed its orbit. She raised an eyebrow. "Reverse polarity," she ordered, and the little earth shot out of the orbital field with the same amazing speed as it had each time she tried the experiment. "Well one must start somewhere. Undo last change," she murmured, and the little earth reappeared in its orbit. "The earth's mass, velocity and the sun's gravitational pull hold it in orbit. We must recalibrate the association in a controlled escape."

As she executed the program to create an electronic grid in a mock-up of the terra-form, she was lost in her thought. "If I can create a bubble around the planet I can create weightlessness," she spoke audibly to herself. "But how would that effectively counteract the sun's pull on the bubble itself? How would it affect velocity?"

She logged and entered each failed equation and started over. Jcarmc knew that the illusive key to the problem was attainable, believing scientific principle would prevail: it always had. She hoped that it would be she who found the key, but would be relieved if any of her contemporaries discovered the solution.

She speculated that the best chance would be to propel the earth out of the galaxy at precisely the right time, and to precisely the correct coordinates to be picked up by Andromeda. Sucaferr maintained that it was next to impossible to calculate the timing over such a tremendous distance. She further contended that the only logical plan involved aiming for the closest of the Megallanic clouds, the satellite galaxies of the Milky Way.

Jcarmc's hypothesis and rebuttal of sucaferr's contention, hinged on the potential instability of the satellite galaxies. All available data indicated that the Milky Way would eventually collide with the Megallanic clouds, which would alter the shape of the galaxy. Andromeda was a fully-developed galaxy, and she was determined to produce proof that it was the only viable choice. She had bits and pieces of the puzzle. She had a vision of what was needed, but how to accomplish her goals eluded her.

After many hours of being totally immersed in grueling research, her focus never wavering, she shoved her chair back, threw both hands up in despair, and snapped, "That's it for now!" Mentally she linked with phigacon and myrmor, "phi, can you and myr come over to my place tonight? I have something to show you. And try to link with jorab and ginchav. I've got to eat and make sure echmol can contain himself; but, there is something that I found in my family lineage and I just want to share. It is superb."

She immediately transported home. While awaiting her dinner, she reminded echmol of his "company manners." She promised a treat if he would recite his "Thou Shalt Nots." He pledged not to pee on the floor, jump on people, lick their faces, bite their ankles, chew on their shoelaces, scratch, lick his privates, sniff their crotches, beg for food, or hurl insults at them. Jcarmc gave her good little dog a new Mylar bone to chew. He didn't want to hurt her feelings, so he accepted it graciously and even wagged his tail a little. Then he hid it in his closet with all the others. They tasted nasty.

Later, after she had given her guests a brief introduction, she intoned, "Hologram; balladeer" and again the simple strains of the stringed instrument accompanied the singer's ballad of devotion and concern. The soft voice began:

"I left Susie's room the way I found it;

I couldn't bring myself to rearrange.

Susie left my heart the way it is and I

Find it impossible to change."

The group sat mesmerized through the entire song. Upon the last note, their voices rose excitedly, "Where did you find that?"

An awed hush enfolded them when jorab repeated jcarmc's instruction, "Hologram; balladeer."

After listening again to the woeful tale, he looked at jcarmc and implored, "Are there any others?"

She replied "Many more."

After an hour or so of listening to this strange, new music the group began to contemplate its origin. "What kind of music is this?" phigacon asked.

"Bluegrass, I think," jcarmc replied.

"What is blue grass?" they all chimed in together, looking at one another quizzically.

"I don't know what the word means, but it is an ancient art form exclusive to the writer's time and culture. The answer sufficed, although most of them would spend the next few days trying to imagine blue grass and what it could possibly have to do with music. Much to jcarmc's delight, they each requested a copy of the entire program, which she promised to provide.

After her friends transported out, jcarmc felt pleased at their enthusiastic response to the music. She told the computer to copy the program and make six disks. Then she invited echmol to join her on her luxurious bed, where they both rested comfortably. Now, that was a treat worth having for a sleepy little dog.

The next day when jcarmc transported herself to work there was a large group of people waiting for her. "Do you have them with you?" they were asking.

"Have what" she replied.

"The disks…copies of the music?"

"Well yes I do, would you all like to hear a song?" their elated chatter echoed into the surrounding corridors.

"Wait please," she laughed, "hologram; balladeer," and again there appeared a singer strumming her guitar. Upon completion of the song jcarmc was amazed and a little scared as the crowd insisted on another song and another. "Please people, we all need to get to work. Let me think today about getting a place where we can enjoy all of these songs," she said loudly. She sighed and leaned against the wall for a moment as they began transporting themselves to their own duty stations.

Once alone, jcarmc wondered aloud how so many people knew. Of course, it was obvious that her friends had told their friends. Nevertheless, it was more than a little disconcerting that there was so much interest. "Phi, are you busy?" jcarmc projected.

"Not too, and I can't tell you how much I enjoyed last night! Thank you, thank you," phi replied.

"That's what I need to talk to you about. A crowd of people showed up here at work to hear the songs, and I told them that we would find a place large enough to hold everyone. Will you help me contact the others and find a place?"

"Of course I will, and you have a good day." Phigacon's abruptness was wrapped in politeness, but jcarmc knew not to annoy her further.

During the afternoon rest period, phigacon contacted jcarmc. She began, "I know the guy who oversees the computer recycling center storage building. He said they just shipped out all of the parts this morning, so the place is empty. Cleaning crews are working on it right now, and he said we can use it this evening."

"That's fast work, phi." Jcarmc continued, "I don't know how to thank you."

"Oh, just keep it as quiet as possible and that will do. I'm not aware of any rules against such public gatherings, but this is out of the ordinary. I mean, it just isn't done. Frankly, I'd rather not have my name stamped all over this."

"I see," jcarmc replied. "I'll contact only the people who were at my house last night, and I'll ask them to bring anyone they've told already, but not to include anyone new."

"Oh, that's a big help," phigacon thought secretly. "Well, I suppose only a few hundred citizens gathering at the recycling plant won't be noticed."

Jcarmc realized that her request had put her friend in a compromising position. More importantly, she recognized that phigacon had just showed the first signs of true emotion in her sarcastic and angry thoughts. She'd have to observe this more closely to see if it might develop into something troublesome.

In the evening, with the appropriate venue provided and jcarmc standing in front of a massive group, the number of which was staggering, she raised a hand and communicated, "Does everyone have his or her recording device?" The gathering returned a deafening "YES!"

"Then please share with those not here, hologram; balladeer, 1 through 18." When the balladeer appeared, no one noticed jcarmc leave the place where she had stood to join the group. Nor did she want them to. About half way through the songs she noticed that she was crying again. She was touched that so many people were enjoying these treasures from her family's past, although they were not as moved as she.

She was startled to feel her molecules began to disperse; yet, it was no surprise when she materialized once again in the Medfour Asian facility.

"Jcarmc" the familiar voice said, "are you still researching your family?"

"Oh please, genphel, not now. My Grandmother is singing for a very large audience."

"How is this possible?" he asked with a puzzled look.

"I'll show you," she said as she grabbed him by the hand and transported both of them back to the holographic concert.

The magic of the music immediately transformed genphel from doctor to fan. He understood more readily why she was so caught up in this pursuit that he had previously considered dangerous. It was when the balladeer was finished and the people were standing and applauding that she realized she was still holding his hand. Quickly she released her clasp and apologized, as he smiled at her glowing cheeks.

Following the concert, an uneventful two days passed; but, on the third, as she was having breakfast, there was a beep on the news screen. She gasped in disbelief at her obituary.

"Jcarmc, Sector 12, Appalachian District. Propagated October 13, 3952. Expiration is scheduled in seven days from first transmission of obituary. After Graduating Global Scientific University at age 7, jcarmc was assigned to the Central Conservatory where she has been instrumental in developing planetary safety protocol.

A replacement has not yet been named, but the announcement is to be forthcoming by the end of the obit-waiting period. She is to be survived by her poodle, echmol, a well-known recording artist. His care and keeping will be reassigned at a later date. Pursuant to the pre-deceased's Declaration of Disposal, the ashes will be introduced into Saturn's rings."

Jcarmc had one week to comply. The coordinates were given so that she could transport herself. The elders deemed this a way to allow the condemned to maintain dignity. Of course, no one ever failed to report, so it was not a matter of necessity to force the issue. Besides, that discreet little computer chip inside the inner thigh made trying to escape an absurd exercise in futility.

Instead of finishing breakfast, she drifted aimlessly about the apartment surveying her belongings, touching some, admiring others. She peeked at echmol in his studio and knew he would be fine. Canines adjust easily, she had read. After a long while of walking, looking, and thinking she realized that she wasn't afraid to die, she just hated to leave. She had so hoped to be involved with the search for the proper solar system in the new galaxy.

She thought for a moment that a week was not enough time to prepare, but immediately realized that there was nothing for her to do, really. The society had taken the burden out of living—and dying. There were no familial relationships; there were very few births and those were selective, and there were no orphans. The causes for greed had been eliminated with the removal of wealth and poverty, so her belongings would revert to the society to be redistributed. She knew that life for everyone would go on, except for jcarmc born 3952 in the Appalachian region of North America.

"Phi can you talk?" She projected.

"Good morning, and how are you?" phigacon replied.

"I received my obituary this morning and I wanted to tell you goodbye before I go down there to see what this is about," jcarmc communicated sincerely.

"Oh dear, there is some mistake, surely," phigacon started.

"I don't think so. I think it's because I refused to abandon my ancestral research."

"Well someone needs to be with you. I'll go!" phigacon offered.

"No please phi, I don't want them to know your name." Jcarmc said, and immediately felt the impact of such a silly statement. Phigacon was over two thousand years old. Because of her important function in balancing the society's budget, almost everyone knew her name. Still the implication was understood and appreciated.

"Well at least keep me informed," phigacon asked.

"I will," jcarmc answered with a calmness that helped her understand the finality of her situation. After she hugged and petted echmol, she took one last look around and said to him, "I'll be gone for awhile so take care of the place for me."

Echmol woofed a half-bark in his abstract way. With a smile for this, the dearest of her friends, she transported to the coordinates given, disappearing from the unobservant echmol.

Jcarmc looked around. The room she stood in had one window, one door. It was all white, walls, ceiling, and floor. It was white. There was one desk and one chair, white of course. "Probably not for me," she murmured as she eyed the straight-backed seat.

Then the door hummed and into the room strode a man considerably taller than she. He wore a blue, one-piece, form-fitted suit. Upon the left breast-section of his garment was the seal of the society, a shimmering, simple adaptation of the ancient symbol for peace.

"What is that thing he's wearing," she thought, "And how did he get into it? Crawl in through the neck?"

She had never seen such a man, his hair was…well, thin, and different colors…black and white. And under his nose was some sinister looking hair. She'd never seen anyone whose hair was like this, and she'd certainly never seen facial hair! She was intimidated and did not want to be in his presence any longer than absolutely necessary.

"So, you're jcarmc," his telepathy was penetrating, and she realized instantly that she could hide nothing from him. "Everyone who works with you tells me that you are a very bright young lady…and if you are, then we should be able to wrap this up very quickly." His gaze was as penetrating as his telepathy and all she could think of was how to get away from him. She nervously bit her lip and felt as though she were going to cry again; but, she was sure that would certainly seal her fate.

"Young lady, you misused your security clearance to obtain documents from the lunar library. I want them returned at once," he said levelly.

What was he talking about she thought, what security clearance? The lunar library was open to everyone. What about the crying? What about the emotions? Wasn't he going to address her emotional transgressions? What was this really all about?

"And all the information you've collected in your family search, you bring that to me. All the manuscripts, the media files, everything." He said. "Do I make myself clear?"

"Yes sir" she muttered, and she was immediately transported back to her place.

Back in her apartment, she stood transfixed for a few seconds pondering her ordeal. His order that she should turn all her information over to him kept echoing in her mind. Well, she couldn't do that. And why was she so intimidated? Suddenly she lost control, all rationality had escaped, and she began to rant and rave at the very brink of hysteria.

"Jcarmc, what a sissy! Why didn't you tell him no? Why didn't you tell him something, anything? What is wrong with you? You are such a…a…girl!"

Her outburst shocked her for she had never spoken to anyone in such a manner, let alone herself. Her awareness shifted to echmol, behind her, barking avidly, jumping with front paws clearing the floor. "And you're not helping!" she shouted at him.

He stopped barking and muttered, "Humans!" and something unintelligible that she was almost sure was obscene, as he turned his back on her, proud nose upturned.

"Careful, I'll wash your mouth out again," she said with a smile. Her mood softened, but the problem still loomed over her as a cloud on the darkest of days.

She transported herself back to where the man sat at the desk writing in a heavy-looking book. "That's odd," she thought, "handwriting has been obsolete for several centuries."

"Yes?" he queried.

"Sir, The things that I've collected, I uh…I won't give them to you. I'll make you a copy of all of it. But they are mine," she said firmly.

"Do you know who you're talking to young lady? I am elanco, one of the oldest people on earth. I have the authority to end your pathetic life here and now," he seethed.

"Yes you do and I certainly don't wish to die, but my music is beautiful and I won't give it up. And killing me won't rid society of it. Everyone who wanted has made a copy for themselves!" She shouted.

"You mean you just gave it away? You just let everyone who heard it make their own copy?" He scorned, "you little fool, the elders should have had this music but you've just given it to everyone. These songs could have profited the society. Now you've ruined that possibility."

"And what would you have me do?" she shot back, "and why do you have hair under you nose? It makes you look evil."

Elanco's furrowed brown smoothed and his lips curled into a mischievous smile. "Evil? I was trying for judicious" he chuckled, "I'll shave it this evening."

"Look jcarmc, if you've given the music away, then that's the way it is. However, we still have an issue. We can't let this continue. Your display of emotions is the real problem. You're losing control, reverting to primitive behavior. We can't have the world as it once was," he urged.

"Now wait a minute, you can't tell me that there's anything wrong with the love that the songs tell about," she returned.

"With the love, no I can't. However, with love comes hate. It seems they're inseparable, at least for our species. And with hate come abuse, captivity, slavery, and sadly even war. Jcarmc you must understand that the society must remain uniform in order to be as pain-free as possible" elanco counseled.

"But it is just music! Just music, yet, it is so different from the music we have," she reflected.

"Tell me about it! We even have canines with their limited vocabulary recording music, if it is indeed music at all. But you see, self-control means that I have the right to turn it off if it offends me, and we encourage that. But most people won't do that with expressionistic music. They listen until it becomes their agenda," he stated.

"But sir, this music is so simple," she started.

Elanco interrupted, "But emotions are not. If you want to research something, then research the society in the twentieth and twenty-first centuries. See for yourself the greed, the inhumanity, the way that people sought revenge, see how governments robbed and enslaved their citizens under the guise of common good. It was a bloody time when children were abused and street gangs terrorized entire neighborhoods. Even all of that paled in comparison to wars! Change had to be made or man would exterminate himself. All of this tragedy and travesty grew from emotions!

We have elders now instead of multiple governments; and, certainly there are no armed forces. Research that, compare the past with the present and come back and tell me how there is no harm in emotions," elanco continued.

Jcarmc could not counter his argument. As she fumbled through her scattered thoughts for just one that made some sense, elanco shocked her out of her daze.

He rose from his seat, speaking with a hint of resignation, "I'm not going to have you put to death, but we do have to stop your ancestral search. You came across the music, it caught your interest, and although it triggered undesirable displays of emotion, this entire affair must stop there. We simply cannot allow you to set a trend. Others may find politics or something else that could ultimately threaten the society and we can't let that happen."

Jcarmc's brain could not filter through anything he had just said except the part about not killing anyone. Her eyebrows pinched close together, she squeaked, "What do you mean you don't have anyone put to death? What about vorbclee and Lisa, poor dear?" she pried.

"I just counseled them, changed their names and moved them to another place. They were not as stubborn as you." His grin began to look so goofy that the "evil" aura vanished.

"What did you change Lisa's name to?" jcarmc asked, so distracted that she couldn't pick up a single thread of the original conversation.

"Lois." At jcarmc's quizzical expression, he shrugged, "Hey, it was her choice." They laughed aloud.

Her mind still tossing about bits and pieces of all the information she was trying to classify, she flitted to another topic, "Why do you write? No one writes anymore? What do you write?"

"Like I said, I'm one of the oldest people on the earth. When I was a child, writing was still taught in school. I like the connection to my own roots. I just never let it get the best of me like your music did to you. As for what I write, well, I write my thoughts, a diary if you please. It doesn't matter what I write, it's just to stay in practice so I don't forget how."

Meandering toward a more lucent plane of thought, she swerved again, "Wait a minute, elanco. There is an elanco in my family line, is that you?" she asked cautiously.

"Yes, I was your donor. I wish I could have been more. I did check on you regularly, and I've wanted to meet you," he confided.

"You mean all of this was just to meet me?" she erupted, anger rising in her voice. She flailed her arms wildly about and paced rapidly back and forth spewing as many accusations per second as her tongue could form. He had let her think she was about to die!

"Certainly not! This is a most serious issue. Your behavior poses a very real danger. Our people are not prepared for the chaos that could ensue if allowed to exhume the psychological relics of our ancestors. Can't you understand the impact of suddenly shattering over 2,000 years worth of careful conditioning? Why, we don't even have police anymore because everyone conforms...or, they are listed in the obits. All we have is a panel of seven elders advising sectors, not armies defending borders. You happen to be in my sector of responsibility. Your transgressions against social tenets could not be ignored."

Jcarmc paled as she envisioned the collapse of society at the hands of a world population reverting to primitive emotions they could never understand. A metamorphosis of her psyche manifested itself in a barely perceptible shudder as she regained control of her emotions.

"Besides, I check on all my children," he grinned.

"All your children?" she baited again.

"Hey, where is it written that position should have no privilege?" Then elanco resumed writing in his book.

"You're just a big phony," she teased.

"Thank you, myrfls" he chuckled again without looking up.